Little Whale

Jo Weaver

Hodder
Children's
Books

Grey Whale led her baby out of the shallows
and into the warm southern sea.

"Where are we going?" asked Little Whale.

"Follow me," said Grey Whale.

The rest of their family had already left to find food in the cool, rich waters of the north. It was time to join them.

"We're going on a long journey, Little Whale,"
sang her mother. "We're going home."

A great forest beneath
them drifted with the tide.

"What's home?" wondered Little Whale.
"Maybe this is it?"

But Grey Whale guided her forward.

The coral reef sparkled
with life. Strange new
creatures swam all
around them.

"Is this home?"
asked Little Whale.

"No, we've still got a long
way to go," said Grey Whale,
nudging her Little Whale onwards.

Together they travelled mile after mile
under vast midnight skies.

Through seas that
shimmered and danced.

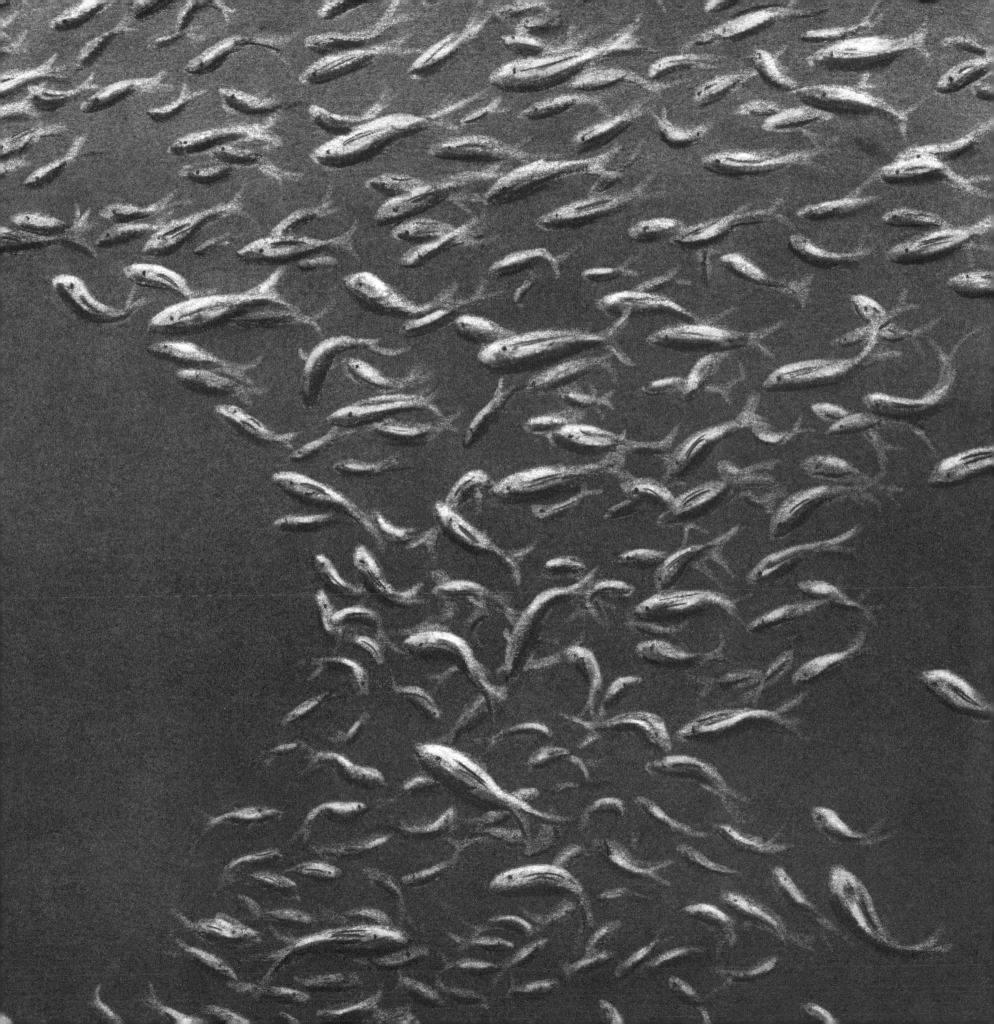

Days and nights passed.
The water grew colder and deeper and darker.

"Are we nearly home yet?" Little Whale asked.

But her voice was lost in the noise of passing ships, and Grey Whale couldn't hear her.

Little Whale felt very small.
There was no one in sight except her mother.

Suddenly they were no longer alone. Orcas were trailing them, and Little Whale knew they were very dangerous.

"I'm scared," she said.

"I'm right beside you, keep going!" urged her mother.

But Little Whale's strength was fading.

"Hold on to me!"
said Grey Whale.

Little Whale clung on to her
mother and they surged through
the water, leaving the danger far behind.

"I'm so tired!" murmured Little Whale.
"Will we ever get there?"

At long last, the sound of whale song
echoed through the icy water.

"Who is that?" asked Little Whale.

"It's our family," said Grey Whale.
"They're calling us home."

Sunshine glittered on the mountain peaks, as the pod
of grey whales sang their welcome.

"We made it! We're home in the north!" said Grey Whale,
and she nuzzled her brave Little Whale.

"So this is it!" said Little Whale. "We're home," she sighed.

Resting safely against the warmth of her mother,
with her family all around her, Little Whale
drifted off to sleep.

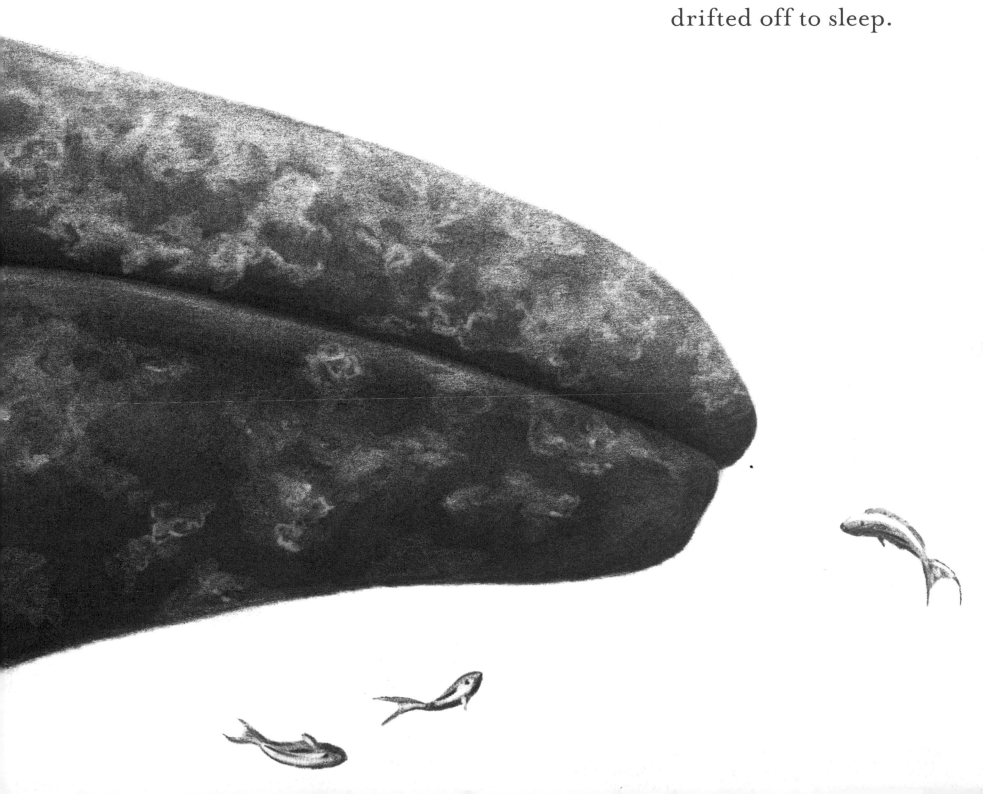

Grey whales migrate up to 12,400 miles every year - a journey which is believed to be the longest annual migration of any mammal. The whales swim south to breed in the late autumn and return to their northern feeding grounds in the spring. Young calves make this epic journey alone with their mother.

For my little artists: Eliza,
Geordie, Jemima, Annie, Raffy,
and Rowan, of course. X

First published in 2018 by Hodder Children's Books
© Jo Weaver 2018

Hodder Children's Books
An imprint of Hachette Children's Group
Part of Hodder & Stoughton
Carmelite House
50 Victoria Embankment
London, EC4Y 0DZ

HB ISBN: 978 1 444 93749 7
PB ISBN: 978 1 444 93750 3

An Hachette UK Company
www.hachette.co.uk

www.hachettechildrens.co.uk